DO NOT ENTER

the Monster ZOO

For Charlie and Martha, and with
special thanks to Julia Churchill – A.S.

For Calum and Angus – S.O.

Amy Sparkes is donating a percentage of her royalties to Tommy's
(registered charity number 1060508). Tommy's exists to save babies' lives through
funding research and providing information. To find out more visit **www.tommys.org**

DO NOT ENTER THE MONSTER ZOO
A RED FOX BOOK 978 1 849 41659 7
Published in Great Britain by Red Fox, an imprint
of Random House Children's Publishers UK
A Random House Group Company
This edition published 2013
3 5 7 9 10 8 6 4
Text copyright © Amy Sparkes, 2013
Illustrations copyright © Sara Ogilvie, 2013
The right of Amy Sparkes and Sara Ogilvie to be identified as the author and illustrator
of this work has been asserted in accordance with the Copyright, Designs and Patents Act 1988.
Red Fox Books are published by Random House Children's Publishers UK,
61–63 Uxbridge Road, London W5 5SA
www.**randomhousechildrens**.co.uk
www.**randomhouse**.co.uk
Addresses for companies within The Random House Group Limited can be found at:
www.randomhouse.co.uk/offices.htm
THE RANDOM HOUSE GROUP Limited Reg. No. 954009
A CIP catalogue record for this book is available from the British Library.
Printed in China

DO NOT ENTER

the Monster ZOO

AMY SPARKES
SARA OGILVIE

RED FOX

One day,

imagine my surprise

to find that
I had won a **prize**!

A note came in the post to say,
"**You** can run the zoo today!"

I grabbed my bike, so keen to go,
and pedalled quickly down the road.

I **whizzed**
through woods,

past hills so green . . .

... to the strangest zoo
I'd **ever** seen!

The Keeper beamed
and skipped to me.
He rubbed his hands
so **gleefully**.

"Please clean the cages, feed the beasts –
they get quite **cross** without their feasts.

Oh dear," he said. "I have a hunch
the Squirgal hasn't had its lunch.
It chews and chumps and chomps a lot,
and **gobbles** children on the spot!

So if you see it, do **take care**.
Its tummy rumbles, so **beware!**"

"I cannot stop – I must away.

Hooray!

Today's my **holiday**!"

Then off he sprinted, with a grin.
I turned the Key and t i p t o e d in . . .

My jaw hit the floor,
my eyes popped **wide** –
I couldn't **believe**
the mess inside!

The naughty creatures stole my hat.
My broom became their **cricket bat**!

And when I went
to clean the floor,

they
kicked

and
flicked . . .

...and **smashed** the door!

They scrambled **high**,
rolled on the ground.

They **howled** and **yowled**
and raced around.

Their hooves
flung **dung**,
and with
their paws

they bent the trees
and **banged** on doors.

Now I'd been left to run this zoo –
but what on earth was I to **do**?

I took my broom, replaced my hat . . .

and loudly said,
"Enough of **that!**"

I grabbed the growling **Grimblegraw**, when from his huge and hairy jaws there came a mighty, frightening **roar**!

His head was high, he looked quite proud,

until I **roared** back twice as loud!

I tracked
the dangling
Dinglebee,

which couldn't
hide as well as me.

I found the **Morph**,

split up the **Quees**,

and caught the **Humple** in the trees.

I jumped up on the **Purple Gurps**.
(I learned to duck their fiery burps!)

I rode till they could run no more –
they slumped back home and shut their door.

I fed the beasts, they **munched** and **crunched**.
I wish that **I** had time for lunch!

A **Flying Flomp**
leapt from a tree,

but couldn't jump as **fast** as me!

The **Furry Furbles** tickled my nose –
I'm glad they have such **ticklish** toes!

But **then** . . .
among the squawks and chirps,
and the fiery burps of the Purple Gurps,
I heard a rumbly tummy **gurgle** . . .

... then I saw the **scary Squirgal!**

It licked its lips quite hungrily,
but I just smiled and said, "You see,
Squirgals are afraid of **me**!
Served with chips, they're really yum.

And, Squirgal,
that gurgle . . .

Just then the Keeper reappeared.
He looked more peaceful,
                    calm and cheered.

"They're good as **gold**!" the Keeper puzzled.
Squirgal purred and Furbles nuzzled.
"Yes," I said and passed the key,
"I soon showed them the boss was **me**!"

The Keeper stared, mouth open wide.
I waved goodbye and began to ride.
I **whizzed** past hills and through the wood . . .
I think today was rather **good**.

Next day, imagine my surprise
to find I'd won **another** prize.
"You've won first place! Well done to you!
Oh, **please** come back and run the zoo!"